EARLY LIGHT

EARLY LIGHT

OSAMU DAZAI

translated from the Japanese
by Ralph McCarthy
& Donald Keene

STORYBOOK ND

PUBLISHER'S NOTE: "Early Light" (Hakumei) and "One Hundred Views of
Mount Fuji" (Fugaku hyakkei) are selected from *Self Portraits*, first published
in 1993 by Kodansha USA, and are published by arrangement with Ralph
McCarthy. "Villon's Wife" (Viyon no tsuma) originally appeared in *New
Directions in Prose and Poetry 15* (New Directions, 1955) and is published by
arrangement with the estate of Donald Keene

Manufactured in the United States of America
First published clothbound by New Directions in 2022

Library of Congress Cataloging-in-Publication Data
Names: Dazai, Osamu, 1909–1948, author. | McCarthy, Ralph F., translator. |
Keene, Donald, translator. | Dazai, Osamu, 1909–1948. Hakumei. English. |
Dazai, Osamu, 1909–1948. Fugaku hyakkei. English. | Dazai, Osamu, 1909–1948.
Viyon no tsuma. English.
Title: Early light / Osamu Dazai ; translated by Ralph McCarthy & Donald Keene.
Other titles: Early light (Compilation)
Description: New York : New Directions Publishing Corporation, 2022. |
Series: A storybook ND
Identifiers: LCCN 2022005823 | ISBN 9780811231985 (hardcover) |
ISBN 9780811232319 (ebook)
Subjects: LCSH: Dazai, Osamu, 1909–1948—Translations into English. |
LCGFT: Short stories.
Classification: LCC PL825.A8 E1713 2022 | DDC 895.63/44—dc23/
eng/20220209
LC record available at https://lccn.loc.gov/2022005823

10 9 8 7 6 5 4 3 2 1

New Directions Books are published for James Laughlin
by New Directions Publishing Corporation
80 Eighth Avenue, NY 10011

EARLY LIGHT

When our house in Mitaka, Tokyo, was damaged in the bombings, we moved to Kōfu, my wife's hometown. Her younger sister had been living alone in the family house there.

This was in early April of 1945. Allied planes passed frequently enough through the skies over Kōfu but hardly ever dropped any bombs. Nor was the war zone atmosphere as intense as it was in Tokyo. We were able to sleep without our air raid gear for the first time in months. I was thirty-seven. My wife was thirty-four, my daughter five, and my son two, technically, though he'd just been born in August of the previous year. Our life up to that point had not been easy by any means, but we had at least remained alive and free of serious illnesses or injuries. Having survived so much adversity, even I felt a desire to go on living a bit longer, if only to see how things would turn out with the world. Stronger than that, however, was the fear that my wife and children would be killed before I was, leaving me alone. Just to think about that possibility was unendurable. I had to see to it that they survived, and that meant adopting the most prudent measures. I had no money, however. Whenever I did get my hands on a fair sum, I would promptly drink it away. I have the serious defect known as a drinking habit. Liquor at that time was an expensive indulgence, but whenever friends or acquaintances visited me, I was unable to stop myself from whisking them off to guzzle great quantities of the stuff, just as I had in the old days.

So much for prudent measures. Even as I envied those who'd long since evacuated their families to the distant countryside, I, for lack of means and out of sheer indolence, remained forever dillydallying in Mitaka, until at last we were visited by a bomb and I lost all desire to stick it out any longer and moved the family to Kōfu. Now, sleeping without my air raid gear for the first time in nearly a hundred days, I was able to breathe a small sigh of relief, reflecting that, though further hardships undoubtedly lay ahead, for the time being at least there'd be no need to bundle up the children in the middle of a cold night and scramble into the bomb shelter.

We were now, however, a family who'd lost their own home, and this put us in an awkward position. I felt as though I'd been through my share of tribulations in life, but moving into someone else's house with two small children in tow allowed me a taste of various distinctive new ones. My wife's mother and father had both passed away, her elder sisters had married and left, and though the youngest of the siblings, a boy, was officially the head of the household, he had entered the navy right after graduating from university two or three years before, leaving the youngest sister, a girl of twenty-six or twenty-seven, alone in the house in Kōfu. She corresponded regularly with her brother, apparently consulting with him in minute detail about all the household affairs. I, of course, was the elder brother-in-law of these two, but, elder or not, I obviously had no voice in managing those affairs. Far from being in a position of authority, in fact, I'd been nothing but a burden to this family ever since my wife and I had married. I was not, in other words, a man to be relied upon. It was only natural, therefore, that I be excluded from consultation, and since I, for my part, had not the slightest interest in the family "assets" or whatever, this was a mutually satisfactory arrangement. But, being older than both the navy boy and his twenty-six or twenty-seven-year-old sister (twenty-eight, maybe—I never really checked), I was worried that we might unintentionally trample on their pride, or that they might be leery of my trying to outsmart them and get my hands on those assets—though surely no one would be *that* distrustful—and the truth is that I felt constantly on guard, as if I were moving through a lush, moss-covered garden, hopping gingerly from one stepping-stone to the next. I even thought how much easier it would be on all of us if only there were a still older man in the house, one who'd accumulated more experience in the real world.

This negative sort of concern for the feelings of others can wear a man out. I borrowed the six-mat room facing the rear garden to work and sleep in and arranged for my wife and children to sleep in the room that housed the Buddhist altar. I paid a fair rent for the rooms and made sure that I contributed our share to the purchase of food and what not, and when I had visitors I took care not to use the parlor, but showed them into my workroom. I am a drinker, however, and visitors from Tokyo were not infrequent, the upshot of which was that, even as I maintained every intention of honoring the privileges due the actual owners of the house, I in fact ended up taking any number of inexcusable liberties. My sister-in-law actually treated us with considerable diffidence and was a great help with the children, but, though there was never an unpleasant, head-on confrontation, we were a family that had lost its home, and while oversensitivity to that fact may have been the true cause of my discomfort, there was, nonetheless, the feeling of forever walking on thin ice. What this all added up to was that, thanks to our evacuation to the country, both the sister and ourselves were put under a debilitating strain. Still, our situation was better than most, it would seem; one can only guess what it was like for those evacuees in even worse circumstances.

"Don't evacuate. Stick it out in Tokyo till your house is burned to the ground: you'll be better off."

I wrote this advice in a letter to a close friend who remained with his family in Tokyo.

We'd come to Kōfu in early April, when it was still chilly and the cherry blossoms, considerably later than those in Tokyo, had just begun to open. We were there throughout May and June, when the heat unique to the Kōfu basin began to make itself felt. The deep green leaves of the pomegranate trees took on an oily sheen in the intense sunlight, and soon their bright red flowers burst into bloom, and the little green grapes grew plumper each day, gradually forming long, rangy bunches that hung heavily from the trellises; and it was just at about that time that a commotion began to sweep through the city of Kōfu. The entire town was abuzz with the rumor that the bombings were to be directed at small and medium-sized cities, and that Kōfu, too, would burn. Everyone began making preparations to flee, loading their carts with household goods and dragging their families off into the mountains; you heard the sounds of footsteps and carts incessantly, even late at night. I had from the beginning been resigned to the fact that Kōfu too would eventually be hit, but to load our belongings on a cart and evacuate to the mountains with my wife and children to beg lodging from strangers when I'd scarcely had time to enjoy the relief of sleeping without air raid gear—that was asking too much.

I thought we should stay where we were. If the incendiary bombs started dropping, my wife, carrying the baby on her back and leading the five-year-old by the hand, could flee to the fields on the outskirts of town while my sister-in-law and I stayed behind and protected the house, fighting the flames as best we could. If it burned down, it burned down; working together, we could build a little shack on the ruins and make our stand.

This was the plan I suggested, and everyone agreed to it. We dug a pit to bury food, a set of kitchen utensils, umbrellas, shoes, toiletries, a mirror, needles and thread—all the barest necessities, to avoid being reduced to utter wretchedness should the house be destroyed.

"Bury these, too." My five-year-old daughter held out a pair of red geta clogs.

"Ah, yes. In they go," I said, taking the clogs and

stuffing them into one corner of the pit. I felt for a moment as if I were burying a person.

"At least now we're all together," my sister-in-law said. She was, perhaps, experiencing the faint glow of happiness one is said to feel on the eve of annihilation. No more than four or five days later, in fact, the house went up in flames. It came a good month earlier than I'd expected.

For the previous ten days or so, the two children had been going to a doctor for eye problems, namely epidemic conjunctivitis, or "pinkeye." The boy's condition wasn't all that bad, but his sister's grew steadily worse. Within about a week—two or three days before the bombing—she had temporarily lost all use of her eyes. Her eyelids were so swollen it distorted her features, and when you forcibly pried the lids apart, you saw an inflamed, festering mess that resembled the eye of a dead fish. Thinking that perhaps this was no mere pinkeye but a virulent bacterial infection of some sort that had already done permanent damage, I took her to a different doctor, but again it was diagnosed as conjunctivitis. It would take quite a while to clear up entirely, we were told, but it would clear up. Doctors frequently make mistakes, however. In fact, they're mistaken more often than not. I've never been one to put undue faith in anything doctors say.

I just hoped she'd regain her eyesight soon. I drank heavily, but couldn't get drunk. One night I even vomited on the way home from a place I'd been drinking at, and I'm not joking when I say that as I squatted there by the roadside I pressed my palms together in prayer. *Please let her eyes be open when I get home.* When I reached the house I heard her singing innocently. Thank God, I thought, dashing inside, only to find her standing there alone with her head bowed in the dimly lit room, singing to herself.

I couldn't bear to watch her. My child went blind because I'm a penniless drunk. If I had led the life of a proper, upstanding citizen, perhaps this calamity would never have occurred. The sins of the father are visited on the child. It was divine retribution. I went so far as to tell myself that if this child's eyes remained closed for the rest of her life, I would give up all thoughts of literature and personal glory to be permanently at her side.

"Where are your footsies, baby? Where are your handsies?" When she was feeling happy she'd play with her baby brother like this, groping for him blindly. What if there were an air raid now, with her in this condition? The thought made me shudder. We'd have no choice but to run for it, with the baby on my wife's back and this child on mine. But it would be impossible for my sister-in-law to protect the house all by herself. She, too, then, would have to flee with us. Judging by what the Allied planes had done to Tokyo, one had to assume that the city of Kōfu would be completely destroyed, including, surely, the doctor's office we were taking the girl to. And the other clinics as well; there wouldn't be a single doctor left in town. Then where would we be?

"I don't care what they do to us. It just seems to me

they might be so kind as to wait another month or so before they do it."

Later on the very night I'd smilingly announced this opinion at the dinner table, we heard the air raid sirens for the first time, simultaneous with the familiar thundering explosions and a lighting up of the sky all around us. They'd begun dropping the incendiary bombs. I heard a series of splashes: my sister-in-law was throwing tableware into the small pond near the veranda.

It was the worst possible time for the attack to come. I boosted my blind child up on my back. My wife did likewise with the baby boy, and we each ran outside clutching a futon. We ran about ten blocks, taking shelter in ditches two or three times along the way, before we came to open fields. No sooner had we spread both futons out on a field of freshly mown barley and sat down to catch our breath than a shower of fire fell from the sky directly overhead.

"Get under the futon!" I shouted to my wife and threw my own futon over me, lying face down with my daughter still clinging to my back. I thought how painful a direct hit would probably be.

We were spared that, but when I threw off the futon and sat up for a look, I saw that we were surrounded by a sea of fire.

"Get up and put out the fire! Put out the fire!" I yelled, not only to my wife but in a voice loud enough for all the others lying on the ground around us to hear, and we began smothering the flames with our mats and blankets. It was almost amusing how easily they went out. Though my daughter could see nothing, she must have sensed that something extraordinary was going on; she clung silently to my shoulders, without uttering so much as a whimper.

"Are you all right?" I asked my wife, walking up to her once the flames were pretty much under control.

"Yes," she said quietly. "Let's hope this is as bad as it gets." For her, apparently, incendiary bombs were nothing compared to the explosive variety.

We moved to another spot in the field to rest, and no sooner had we done so than it began to rain fire again. This may sound strange, but it occurred to me that perhaps there is a splinter of divinity in each of us after all. Not only our family but everyone who'd taken refuge in that field escaped injury. We all busied ourselves snuffing out the sticky, greasy, flaming globs with futons or blankets or dirt, then sat back down to rest.

My sister-in-law left for the house of a distant relative in the hills some four miles from the city to try to get food for the following day. My wife and the children and I sat on one of the futons and used the other to cover ourselves. We decided this was as good a place as any to hold our ground. I was exhausted. I'd had just about enough of running hither and thither with the girl on my back. The children were now lying quietly on the futon, asleep, while their parents gazed vacantly at the glow of Kōfu going up in flames. The roar of the airplanes had decreased considerably.

"I guess it's about over," my wife said.

"Yeah. Well, none too soon for me, I'll tell you."

"I suppose the house burned down."

"Well, you never know. It'd be nice if it was still there."

I figured it was hopeless, but wouldn't it be wonderful if by some miracle the house was still standing?

"Not likely, though," I said.

"No, I suppose not."

It was hard to abandon the last flicker of hope, however.

A farmhouse was blazing away right before us. It took an incredibly long time to burn to the ground. One could almost see the history of that house going up in flames along with its roof and pillars.

The night faded into a pale dawn.

We carried the children to the national school, which hadn't burned. They let us rest in a classroom on the second floor. The children began to wake. Even after waking up, of course, the girl's eyes remained closed. Groping about, she amused herself by climbing up on the lecturer's platform and what not. Her condition seemed scarcely to weigh on her mind.

I left the wife and children there and set out to check on the house. It was a tremendous ordeal just walking through the streets, what with the heat and smoke from the smoldering houses on either side, but by following a roundabout path, changing course any number of times, I somehow managed to reach our neighborhood. How happy I would be if the house were still standing! But, no, it couldn't possibly be. I told myself I shouldn't get my hopes up, but the phantom of that one-in-a-million chance kept raising its head. I came in sight of the black wooden fence around the house.

It was still there!

But it was only the fence. The house itself was completely destroyed. My sister-in-law was standing in the ruins, her face black with soot.

"Hi. How are the children?"

"They're fine."

"Where are they?"

"At the school."

"I've got some riceballs. I had to walk like mad, but at least I got some food."

"Thanks."

"Let's keep our spirits up. Look at this. Most of the things we buried are fine. We'll be all right for the time being."

"We should have buried more stuff."

"It's all right. With all this, we'll be able to hold our heads up high wherever we go for help. I'm going to take some food to the school. You stay here and rest. Here, have some riceballs. Take as many as you like."

A woman of twenty-seven or twenty-eight is in some ways more mature than a man of forty or more. She was a rock, a model of composure. Her perfectly worthless brother-in-law proceeded to rip a few planks from the fence, lay them on the ground in the field in back, and sit down with legs crossed to stuff his cheeks with the riceballs she'd left. I was completely without resources or plan. But, whether good for nothing or just plain stupid, I didn't give a thought to what we were to do. The only thing that really concerned me was my daughter's eye problem. How in the world would we go about treating it now?

Before very long my wife and sister-in-law arrived. My wife had the baby on her back, and my sister-in-law was leading my daughter by the hand.

"Did you walk all the way here?" I asked my daughter.

"Uh-huh," she said, nodding.

"Is that right? That's really something. The house burned down."

"Uh-huh." She nodded again.

"It looks like the doctor's place is gone, too," I said, turning to my wife. "What are we going to do about her eyes?"

"We had them washed out this morning."

"Where?"

"A doctor came by the school."

"Really? That's great."

"No, just the best they could do. A nurse did it."

"Oh."

We took shelter for the day at the house of a schoolfriend of my sister-in-law's on the outskirts of town. With us we carried the food and the pots and pans we'd unearthed from the pit. Smiling at my sister-in-law, I pulled a watch from my pocket.

"We've still got this. I grabbed it before I ran out of the house."

It was my brother-in-law's pocket watch. I'd found it in the desk some time before and taken it out for my own use.

"Good going." She smiled back at me. "You surprise me. This really adds to our assets."

I was rather proud of myself. "It can be pretty inconvenient if you don't have a timepiece, you know." I pressed the watch into my little girl's hand. "See?" I said. "It's a watch. Put it up to your ear. Hear it go tick-tick-tick? Look at that," I told my wife and her sister. "It even makes a good toy for blind kids."

My daughter was standing perfectly still with her head cocked and the watch pressed against her ear when suddenly it slipped from her hand. It made a clear, tinkling sound as it hit the ground. The crystal was smashed to pieces. It was beyond repair. One could hardly expect to find a shop selling watch crystals.

"Oh, no," I said, my heart sinking.

"Dummy," my sister-in-law muttered, but I was relieved to see that she didn't seem particularly distressed about suddenly losing what was virtually the only "asset" she had left.

We cooked dinner in a corner of the garden at the schoolfriend's house, then retired early in a six-mat room inside. My wife and her sister, tired as they were, seemed unable to sleep and were quietly discussing what we should do.

"Hey, there's nothing to worry about," I told them. "We'll all go to my family's place up north. Everything's going to be fine."

They fell silent. From the beginning, neither of them had put much stock in any opinions of mine. They were apparently devising plans of their own now and didn't even deign to reply.

"All right, I know you don't have any faith in me." I smiled sourly. "But, listen, trust me just this once. That's all I'm asking."

I heard my sister-in-law giggle in the darkness, as if I'd said something totally outlandish. Then she and my wife continued their discussion.

"Fine. Suit yourselves," I said with a chuckle of my own. "Not much I can do if you won't trust in me."

"Well, what do you expect?" my wife suddenly snapped. "You say such preposterous things, we never know if you're joking or serious. It's only natural that we don't rely on you. Even now, with things the way they are, I bet all you can think about is sake."

"Don't be ridiculous."

"But if we had some, you'd drink it, wouldn't you?"

"Well, I don't know, maybe I would."

The two ladies decided that, at any rate, it wouldn't do to impose on our present hosts any more than we already had, and that, come morning, we'd have to look for somewhere else to stay. The following day we loaded our things on a large cart and went to the house of another of my sister-in-law's acquaintances. This house was quite a spacious affair. The man who owned it was about fifty and seemed a gentleman of sterling character. He lent us a ten-mat room. We also found a hospital nearby. The gentleman's wife told us that the prefectural hospital in Kōfu had been destroyed and had relocated to a building here on the outskirts of town. My wife and I each shouldered a child and set out, taking a shortcut through the mulberry fields, and reached the hospital, at the foot of the mountains, in about ten minutes.

The opthalmologist was a woman.

"The girl can't open her eyes at all. We're thinking about heading for my family's house in the country, but it's a long trip by train, and we don't even want to attempt it if her condition might get worse on the way. We're really at our wits' end." Wiping the sweat from my face, I fervently described the girl's symptoms, hoping to induce the lady doctor to do everything in her power to help us.

"What, this?" she said breezily. "This will clear up in no time."

"Really?"

"It hasn't affected the eyes themselves at all. I'm sure you'll be able to travel in four or five days."

My wife broke in to ask if there were any injections that could be given for this sort of thing.

"There are, yes, but ..."

"Please, Doctor," said my wife, bowing deeply.

Whether the injection worked or the infection had simply run its natural course I couldn't say, but my daughter's eyes opened on the afternoon of the second day after we visited the hospital.

"Thank goodness, thank goodness," was all I could say, and I said it over and over. The first thing I did was take her to see what was left of the house.

"See? It burned all up."

"Yeah," she said, with a big smile on her face. "Burned all up."

"Everything's gone. Mr. Rabbit, our shoes, the Oda-giri house, the Chino house, they all burned up."

"Yeah, they all burned up," she said, still smiling.

TRANSLATED BY RALPH McCARTHY

ONE HUNDRED VIEWS
OF MOUNT FUJI

The slopes of Hiroshige's Mount Fuji converge at an angle of eighty-five degrees, and those in Bunchō's paintings at about eighty-four, but if you study survey maps drawn by the army, you'll find that the angle formed by the eastern and western slopes is one hundred twenty-four degrees, and that formed by the northern and southern slopes is one hundred seventeen. And it's not only Hiroshige and Bunchō—most paintings of Fuji, in fact, depict the slopes meeting at an acute angle, the summit slender, lofty, delicate. Some of Hokusai's renditions fairly resemble the Eiffel Tower, peaking at nearly thirty degrees. But the real Fuji is unmistakably obtuse, with long, leisurely slopes; by no means do one hundred twenty-four degrees east-west and one hundred seventeen north-south make for a very steep peak. If I were living in India, for example, and were suddenly snatched up and carried off by an eagle and dropped on the beach at Numazu in Japan, I doubt if I'd be very much impressed at the sight of this mountain. Japan's "Fujiyama" is "wonderful" to Westerners simply because they've heard so much about it and yearned so long to see it; but how much appeal would Fuji hold for one who's never been exposed to such popular propaganda, for one whose heart is simple and pure and free of preconceptions? It would, perhaps, strike that person as almost pathetic, as mountains go. It's short. In relation to the width of its base, quite short. Any mountain with a base that size should be at least half again as tall.

The only time Fuji looked really tall to me was when I saw it from Jukkoku Pass. That was good. At first, because it was cloudy, I couldn't see the top, but I judged from the angle of the lower slopes and picked out a spot amid the clouds where I thought the peak probably was, only to find, when the sky began to clear, that I was way off. The bluish summit loomed up twice as high as I'd expected. I was not so much surprised as strangely tickled, and I cackled with laughter. I had to hand it to Fuji that time. When you come face to face with absolute reliability, you tend, first of all, to burst into silly laughter. You just come all undone. It's like—this is a funny way to put it, I know, but it's like chuckling with relief after loosening your belt. Young men, if ever the one you love bursts out laughing the moment she sees you, you are to be congratulated. By no means must you reproach her. She has merely been overwhelmed by the absolute reliability she senses in you.

Fuji from the window of an apartment in Tokyo is a painful sight. In winter it's quite clear and distinct. That small white triangle poking up over the horizon: that's Fuji. It's nothing; it's a Christmas candy. What's more, it lists pathetically to the left, like a battleship slowly beginning to founder. It was during the winter three years ago that a certain person caught me off guard with a shocking confession. I was at my wits' end. That night I sat alone in one room of my apartment, guzzling sake. I drank all night, without sleeping a wink. At dawn I went to relieve myself, and through the wire mesh screen covering the square window in the toilet I could see Fuji. Small, pure white, leaning slightly to the left: that's one Fuji I'll never forget. On the asphalt street below the window, a fishmonger sped by on his bicycle, muttering to himself ("You can sure see Fuji good this morning ... Damn, it's cold ..."), and I stood in the dark little room, stroking the mesh screen and weeping with despair. That's an experience the like of which I hope never to go through again.

In the early autumn of 1938, determined to rethink my life, I packed a single small valise and set out on a journey.

Kōshū. What distinguishes the mountains here is their gentle and strangely aimless rise and fall. A man named Kojima Usui once wrote, in *The Landscape of Japan,* that "to these mountains come many cross-grained, self-willed sorts to disport themselves like wizard monks." As mountains go, these are, perhaps, freaks. I boarded a bus in Kōfu City and arrived, after a boneshaking, hour-long ride, at Misaka Pass.

Misaka Pass: one thousand three hundred meters above sea level. At the top of the pass is Tenka Chaya, a small teahouse, in a room on the second floor of which my mentor Ibuse Masuji had been holed up writing since early summer. I'd come with the knowledge that I'd find him here. Provided it wouldn't be a hindrance to his work, I, too, intended to rent a room in the teahouse and do a bit of disporting amid those mountains.

Mr. Ibuse was hard at work. I received his permission and settled in, and spent each day from then on, like it or not, face to face with Fuji. This pass, once a strategic point on the road to Kamakura that connected Kōfu with the Tokaido Highway, offers a prospect of the northern slope that has been counted as one of the Three Great Views of Mount Fuji since ancient times. Far from being pleased with the view, however, I found myself holding it in contempt. It's too perfect. You have Fuji right before you and, lying at its feet, the cold, white expanse of Lake Kawaguchi cradled by hushed, huddling mountains on either side. One look threw me into blushing confusion. It was a wall painting in a public bath. Scenery on a stage. So precisely made to order it was mortifying to behold.

On a sunny afternoon two or three days after I'd arrived, when Mr. Ibuse had caught up on his work somewhat, we hiked up to Mitsu Pass together. Mitsu Pass: one thousand seven hundred meters above sea level. A bit higher than Misaka Pass. You reach the top after climbing a steep slope, more or less on all fours, for about an hour. Parting the ivies and vines as I half crawled toward the summit, I presented a spectacle that was far from lovely. Mr. Ibuse was in proper hiking clothes and cut a jaunty figure, but I, having no such gear, was clad in a *dotera*—a square-cut, padded cotton kimono—that the teahouse had provided me with. It was too short and left a stretch of hairy shin exposed on either leg. I was also wearing a pair of thick, rubber-soled work-shoes lent me by an old man at the teahouse, and was acutely aware of how shabby I looked. I'd made a few adjustments, securing the dotera with a narrow, manly sash and donning a straw hat I'd found hanging on the wall, but the only result was that I looked even more bizarre. I'll never forget how Mr. Ibuse, a person who would never stoop to belittling someone's appearance, eyed me with a compassionate air and tried to console me by muttering something about it not becoming a man, after all, to concern himself very much with fashion.

At any rate, we eventually reached the top, but no sooner had we done so than a thick fog rolled over us, and even standing on the observation platform at the edge of the cliff provided us with no view whatsoever. We couldn't see a thing. Enveloped in that dense fog, Mr. Ibuse sat down on a rock, puffed slowly at a cigarette, and broke wind. He looked decidedly out of sorts. On the observation platform were three somber little teahouses. We chose one that was run by an elderly couple and had a cup of hot green tea. The old woman felt sorry for us and said what a stroke of bad luck the fog was, that it would surely clear before long, that normally you could see Fuji right there, looming up before you, plain as day. She then retrieved a large photograph of the mountain from the interior of the teahouse and carried it to the edge of the cliff, held it high in both hands, and earnestly explained that you could generally see Fuji just here, just like this, this big and this clear. We sipped at the coarse tea, admiring the photo and laughing. That was a fine Fuji indeed. We ended up not even regretting the impenetrable fog.

It was, I believe, two days later that Mr. Ibuse left Misaka Pass, and I accompanied him as far as Kōfu. In Kōfu I was to be introduced to a certain young lady whom Mr. Ibuse had suggested I marry. Mr. Ibuse was dressed casually, in his hiking clothes. I wore a kimono and a thin summer coat secured with my narrow sash. He led me to the young lady's house on the outskirts of the city. A profusion of roses grew in the garden. The young lady's mother showed us into the parlor, where we exchanged greetings, and after a while the young lady came in. I didn't look at her face. Mr. Ibuse and the mother were carrying on a desultory, grown-up conversation when, suddenly, he fixed his eye on the wall above and behind me and muttered, "Ah, Fuji." I twisted around and looked up at the wall. Hanging there was a framed aerial photograph of the great crater atop the mountain. It resembled a pure white waterlily. After studying the photo, I slowly twisted back to my original position and glanced fleetingly at the girl. That did it. I made up my mind then and there that, though it might entail a certain amount of difficulty, I wanted to marry this person. That was a Fuji I was grateful for.

Mr. Ibuse returned to Tokyo that day, and I went back to Misaka Pass. Throughout September, October, and the first fifteen days of November I stayed on the second floor of the teahouse, pushing ahead with my work a little at a time and trying to come to terms with that Great View of Fuji until it all but did me in.

I had a good laugh one day. A friend of mine, a member of "The Japan Romantics" who was then lecturing at a university or something, dropped by the teahouse during a hiking excursion, and the two of us stepped into the corridor on the second floor to smoke and poke fun at the view of Fuji we had through the windows there.

"Awfully, crass, isn't it? It's like, 'Ah, Honorable Mount Fuji.'"

"I know. It's embarrassing to look at."

"Say, what's that?" my friend said suddenly, gesturing with his chin. "That fellow dressed up like a monk."

A small man of about fifty, wearing a ragged black robe and dragging a long staff, was climbing toward the pass, turning time and again to gaze up at Fuji.

"It reminds you of that painting *Priest Saigyō Admiring Mount Fuji*, doesn't it?" I said. "The fellow has a lot of style." To me the monk seemed a poignant evocation of the past. "He might be some great saint or something."

"Don't be absurd," my friend said with cold detachment. "He's a common beggar."

"No, no. There's something special about him. Look how he walks—he's got style, I tell you. You know, they say the priest Noin used to write poems praising Fuji right here on this pass, and—"

I was interrupted by my friend's laughter. "Ha! Look at that. You call that 'having style'?"

Hachi, my hosts' pet dog, had begun to bark at Noin, throwing him into a panic. The scene that ensued was painfully ludicrous.

"I guess you're right," I said, crestfallen.

The beggar's panic increased until he began to flounder disgracefully about, threw away his staff, and finally ran for dear life. It was true, he had no style at all. Our priest was as crass as his Fuji, we decided, and even now, thinking back on that scene, it strikes me as laughably absurd.

A courteous and affable young man of twenty-five named Nitta came to visit me at the teahouse. He worked in the post office in Yoshida, a long, narrow town that lies at the base of the mountains below the pass, and said he'd learned where I was by seeing mail addressed to me. After we'd talked in my room for a while and had begun to feel at ease with each other, he smiled and said, "Actually, I was going to come with two or three of my friends, but at the last moment they all pulled out, and, well, I read something by Satō Haruo-sensei that said you were terribly decadent, and mentally disturbed to boot, so I could hardly force them to come. I had no idea you'd be such a serious and personable gentleman. Next time I'll bring them. If it's all right with you, of course."

"It's all right, sure." I forced a smile. "But let me get this straight. You came here on a sort of reconnaissance mission on behalf of your friends, summoning up every ounce of courage you could muster, is that it?"

"A one-man suicide corps," Nitta candidly replied. "I

read Satō-sensei's piece again last night and resigned myself to various possible fates."

I was looking at Fuji through the window. Fuji stood there impassive and silent. I was impressed.

"Not bad, eh? There's something to be said for Fuji after all. It knows what it's doing." It occurred to me that I was no match for Fuji. I was ashamed of my own fickle, constantly shifting feelings of love and hatred. Fuji was impressive. Fuji knew what it was doing.

"It knows what it's doing?" Nitta seemed to find my words odd. He smiled sagaciously.

Whenever Nitta came to visit me from then on, he brought various other youths with him. They were all quiet types. They called me "Sensei," and I accepted that with a straight face. I have nothing worth boasting about. No learning to speak of. No talent. My body's a mess, my heart impoverished. Only the fact that I've known suffering, enough suffering to feel qualified to let these youths call me "Sensei" without protesting— that's all I have, the only straw of pride I can cling to. But it's one I'll never let go of. A lot of people have written me off as a spoiled, selfish child, but how many really know how I've suffered inside?

Nitta and a youth named Tanabe, who was skilled at composing tanka poems, were readers of Mr. Ibuse's work, and perhaps because of this they were the ones I felt most comfortable with and became closest to. They took me to Yoshida once. It was an appallingly long and narrow town, dominated by the mountains that loomed above. Cut off from the sun and wind by Fuji, it was dark and chilly and not unlike the meandering, spindly stem of a light-starved plant. Streams flowed alongside the streets. This is characteristic, apparently, of towns at the foot of mountains; in Mishima, too, steadily flowing streams are everywhere, and people there sincerely believe that the water comes from the snows melting on Fuji. Yoshida's streams are shallower and narrower than those in Mishima, and the water is dirtier. I was looking down at one of them as I spoke:

"There's a story by Maupassant about a maiden somewhere who swims across a river each night to meet some young scion of the nobility, but I wonder what she did about her clothes. Surely she wouldn't have gone to meet him in the nude?"

"No, surely not." The young men thought it over. "Maybe she had a bathing suit."

"Do you suppose she might've piled her clothes on top of her head and tied them down before she started swimming?"

The youths laughed.

"Or maybe she swam in her clothes, and when she met the scion she'd be soaking wet, and they'd sit by the stove till she dried. But then what would she do on the way back? She'd have to get the clothes all wet again swimming home. I worry about her. I don't see why the young nobleman doesn't do the swimming. A man can swim in just a pair of shorts without looking too ridiculous. Do you suppose the scion was one of those people who swim like a stone?"

"No," Nitta said earnestly. "I think it was just that the maiden was more in love than he was."

"You may be right. The maidens in foreign stories are cute like that—very daring. I mean, if they love somebody, they'll even swim across a river to meet him. You won't see that in Japan. Just think of … what was the title of that play? In the middle there's a river, and on one bank stands a man and on the other a princess, and they spend the whole play weeping and moaning. There's no need for the princess to carry on like that. Why doesn't she just swim to the other side? When you see it on stage, it's a very narrow river—she could probably wade across. All that crying is pointless. She won't get any sympathy from me. Now, in the *Asagao Diary* it's the Ōi River—that's a big river, and Asagao is blind, so you feel for her to some extent, but, even so, it's not as if it'd be impossible for her to swim across. Hanging on to some piling beside the river, ranting and blaming it all on the sun—what good is that going to do? Ah, wait a minute. There was one daring maiden in Japan. She was something. You know who I mean?"

"Who?" The young men's eyes lit up.

"Lady Kiyo. She swam the Hidaka River, chasing after the monk Anchin. Swam like hell. She was something, I tell you, and according to a book I read she was only fourteen at the time."

We walked along the road chattering drivel like this until we came to a quiet old inn on the outskirts of town that was run by an acquaintance of Tanabe's.

We drank there, and Fuji was good that night. At about ten o'clock, the youths left me at the inn and returned to their homes. Rather than going to sleep,

I walked outside in my dotera. The moon was astonishingly bright. Fuji was good. Bathed in moonlight, it was a nearly translucent blue, and I felt as if I'd fallen under the spell of a sorcerer fox. Such a sparkling, vivid blue. Like phosphorus burning. Will-o'-the-wisp. Foxfire. Fireflies. Eulalia. Kuzu-no-Ha, the white fox in human form. I followed the road, walking a perfectly straight line, though I could have sworn I had no legs. There was only the sound of my geta clogs—a sound that had nothing to do with me but was, rather, like a separate living thing—reverberating with exceptional clarity: *clatter, clop, clatter, clop.* Stealthily I turned to look back. Fuji was there, burning blue and floating in space. I sighed. A valiant Meiji Royalist. Kurama Tengu. That's how I saw myself. I rather cockily folded my arms and marched on, convinced I was an awfully dashing fellow. I walked quite a long way. I lost my coin purse. It held about twenty silver fifty-sen pieces—it was heavy and must have slipped from the folds of my dotera. I was strangely indifferent. If my money was gone, all I had to do was walk to Misaka Pass. I kept walking. At some point, though, it occurred to me that if I retraced my steps I'd find my purse. Arms folded, I ambled back the way I'd come. Fuji. The Meiji Royalist. A lost coin purse. It all made, I thought, for a fascinating romance. My purse lay glittering in the middle of the road. Of course; where else would it be? I picked it up, returned to the inn, and went to bed.

I'd been bewitched by Fuji that night, transformed into a simpleton, a mooncalf, completely without a will of my own. Even now, recalling it all leaves me feeling peculiarly weary and languid.

I stayed in Yoshida just one night. When I got back to Misaka Pass, the woman who ran the place was all knowing smiles, and her fifteen-year-old sister was standoffish. I found myself wanting to assure them I'd been up to nothing naughty, and, though they asked me no questions, I related in detail my experiences of the previous day. I told them everything—the name of the inn I'd stayed at, how Yoshida's sake tasted, how Fuji looked in the moonlight, how I'd dropped my purse. The little sister seemed appeased.

"Get up and look, sir!" One morning not long afterwards, this same girl stood outside the teahouse shouting up to me in a shrill voice, and I grudgingly got up and stepped out into the corridor.

Her cheeks were flushed with excitement. She said nothing, only pointed toward the sky. I looked, and— ah!—snow. Snow had fallen on Fuji. The summit was a pure and radiant white. Not even the Fuji from Misaka Pass is to be scoffed at, I thought.

"Looks good," I said.

"Isn't it superb?" she said, triumphantly selecting a better word. She squatted down on her heels and said, "Do you still think Misaka's Fuji is hopeless?"

I'd often lectured the girl to the effect that this Fuji was hopelessly vulgar, and perhaps she'd taken it more to heart than I'd realized.

"Let's face it," I said, amending my teaching with a grave countenance. "Fuji is just no good without snow."

In my dotera I walked about the mountainside filling both my hands with evening primrose seeds, which I brought back to the teahouse and scattered in the back yard.

"Now, listen," I said to the girl, "these are *my* evening primroses, and I'm coming back next year to see them, so I don't want you throwing out your laundry water and whatnot here." She nodded.

I'd chosen this particular flower because a certain incident had convinced me that Fuji goes well with evening primroses. The teahouse at Misaka Pass is what one might call remote, so much so that mail isn't even delivered there. Thirty minutes' bouncing and swaying on a bus brings you to the foot of the pass and Kawaguchi, a poor little village if ever there was one, on the shore of the lake; it was at the post office here that my mail was held for me, and once every three days or so I had to make the journey to pick it up. I tried to choose days when the weather was good. The girl conductors on the buses don't offer the sightseers aboard much in the way of information about the scenery. But once in a while, almost as an afterthought, in listless near-mumble, one of them will come out with something dreadfully prosaic like: "That's Mitsu Pass; over there is Lake Kawaguchi; freshwater smelt inhabit the lake."

Having claimed my mail one day, I was riding the bus back to Misaka Pass, sitting next to a woman of about sixty who wore a dark brown coat over her kimono, whose face was pale and nicely featured, and who looked a lot like my mother, when the girl conductor suddenly said, as if it had just occurred to her, "Ladies and gentlemen, you can certainly see Fuji clearly today, can't you?"—words that could be construed as neither information nor spontaneous exclamation. All the passengers—among them young salaried workers with rucksacks, and silk-clad geisha types with hair piled high in the traditional style and handkerchiefs pressed fastidiously to their lips—simultaneously twisted in their seats and craned their necks to gaze out the windows at that commonplace triangle of a mountain as if seeing it for the first time and to ooh and ah like idiots, briefly filling the bus with a buzzing commotion. Unlike all the other passengers, however, the elderly person next to me, looking as though she harbored some deep anguish in her heart, didn't so much as glance at Fuji, but stared out the opposite window at the cliff that bordered the road. Observing this, I felt a sense of almost benumbing pleasure and a desire to show her that I, too, in my refined, nihilistic way, had no interest in ogling some vulgar mountain like Fuji, and that, though she wasn't asking me to, I sympathized with her and well understood her suffering and misery. As if hoping to receive the old woman's motherly affection and approval, I quietly sidled closer and sat gazing vacantly out at the cliff with her.

Perhaps she felt somehow at ease with me. "Ah! Evening primroses," she said absently, pointing a slender finger at a spot beside the road. The bus passed quickly on, but the petals of the single golden evening primrose I'd glimpsed remained vivid in my mind.

Facing up admirably to all 3,778 meters of Mount Fuji, not wavering in the least, erect and heroic—I feel almost tempted to say Herculean—that evening primrose was good. Fuji goes well with evening primroses.

Mid-October came and went, and I was still making very little progress with my work. I missed people. Sunset brought scarlet-rimmed clouds with undersides like the bellies of geese, and I stood alone in the corridor on the second floor smoking cigarettes, intentionally not looking at Fuji, my eyes fixed instead on the autumn leaves of the mountain forests, crimson as dripping blood. I called to the proprietress of the teahouse, who was sweeping up fallen leaves in front.

"Good weather tomorrow, Missus!"

Even I was surprised by the shrillness of my voice; it sounded almost like a cry of joy. She rested her hands on the broom a moment and looked up at me dubiously, knitting her brow.

"Did you have something special planned for tomorrow?"

She had me there.

"No. Nothing."

She laughed. "You must be getting lonesome. Why don't you go mountain climbing or something?"

"Climb a mountain and you just have to come right back down again. It's so pointless. And whatever mountain you climb, what is there to see but the same old Mount Fuji? The heart grows heavy just thinking about it."

I suppose it was a strange thing to say. The proprietress merely nodded ambiguously and carried on sweeping the fallen leaves.

Before going to sleep I would quietly open the curtains in my room and look through the glass at Fuji. On moonlit nights it was a pale, bluish white, standing there like the spirit of the rivers and lakes. I'd sigh. Ah, I can see Fuji. How big the stars are. Fine weather tomorrow, no doubt. These were the only glimmerings I had of the joy of being alive, and after quietly closing the curtains again I'd go to bed and reflect that, yes, the weather would be fine tomorrow—but so what? What did that have to do with me? It would strike me as so absurd that I'd end up chuckling wryly to myself as I lay on my futon.

It was excruciating. My work … Not so much the torment of simply dragging pen over paper (not that at all, in fact, since the writing itself is actually something I take pleasure in), but the interminable wavering and agonizing over my view of the world, and what we call art, and the literature of tomorrow, the search for something new, if you will—questions like these left me quite literally writhing in anguish.

To take what is simple and natural—and therefore succinct and lucid—to snatch hold of that and transfer it directly to paper, was, it seemed to me, everything, and that thought sometimes allowed me to see the figure of Fuji in a different light. Perhaps, I would think, that shape was in fact a manifestation of the beauty of what I like to think of as "elemental expression." Thus I'd find myself on the verge of coming to an understanding with this Fuji, only to reflect that, no, there was something about it, something in its exceedingly cylindrical simplicity that was too much for me, that if this Fuji was worthy of praise, then so were figurines of the Laughing Buddha—and I find figurines of the Laughing Buddha insufferable, certainly not what anyone could call expressive. And the figure of this Fuji, too, was somehow mistaken, somehow wrong, I would think, and once again I'd be back where I started, confused.

Mornings and evenings gazing at Fuji: that's how I spent the cheerless days. In late October, a group of prostitutes from Yoshida, on what, for all I knew, may have been their only day of freedom in the year, arrived at Misaka Pass in five automobiles. I watched them from the second floor. In a flurry of colors, the girls fluttered out of the cars like carrier pigeons dumped out of baskets, and, not knowing at first in which direction to head, flocked together, fidgeting and jostling one another in silence, until at last their curious nervousness began to dissipate, and one by one they wandered off their separate ways. Some meekly chose picture postcards from a rack at the front of the teahouse; others stood gazing at Fuji. It was a dismal and all but unwatchable scene. Though I, a solitary man on the second floor, might feel for those girls to the extent that I'd be willing to die for them, there was nothing I could offer them in the way of happiness. All I could do was look helplessly on. Those who suffer shall suffer. Those who fall shall fall. It had nothing to do with me, it was just the way the world was. Thus I forced myself to affect indifference as I gazed down at them, but it was still more than a little painful.

Let's appeal to Fuji. The idea came to me suddenly. Hey, look out for these girls, will you? Inwardly muttering the words, I turned my gaze toward the mountain, standing tall and impassive against the wintry sky and looking for all the world like the Big Boss, squared off in an arrogant pose, arms folded. Greatly relieved, I forsook the band of courtesans and set out in a light-hearted mood for the tunnel down the road with the six-year-old boy from the teahouse and the shaggy dog, Hachi. Near the entrance to the tunnel, a skinny prostitute of about thirty stood by herself silently gathering a bouquet of some dreary sort of wildflowers. She didn't so much as turn to glance at us as we passed but continued picking the flowers intently. Look after this one, too, I prayed, casting an eye back at Fuji and pulling the little boy along by his hand as I walked briskly into the tunnel. Reminding myself it all had nothing to do with me, I strode resolutely on as the cold water that seeped through the ceiling dripped down on my cheeks and the back of my neck.

It was at about that time that my wedding plans met with a serious hitch. I was given to understand, in no uncertain terms, that my family back home was not going to lend their assistance. Once married, I fully intended to support my household with my writing, but I had been selfish and presumptuous enough to assume that my family would, at this juncture, come to my aid to the tune of at least a hundred yen or so, allowing me to have a dignified, if modest, wedding ceremony. After an exchange of two or three letters, however, it became clear that this would not be the case, and I was thoroughly at a loss as to what to do. Having come to terms with the fact that, as things stood, it was entirely possible that the young lady's side would call the whole thing off, I decided there was nothing for it but to make a clean breast of everything, and came down from the mountain alone to call at the house in Kōfu. I was shown into the parlor, where I sat facing the girl and her mother and told them all. At times it sounded, disconcertingly enough, as if I were reciting a speech. But I thought I at least managed to describe the situation in a relatively straightforward and honest manner.

The young lady remained calm. "Does that mean your family is opposed to the idea?" she asked, tilting her head to one side.

"No, it's not that they're opposed." I pressed softly down on the table with the palm of my right hand. "It just seems to be their way of telling me I'm on my own."

"Then there's no problem." The mother smiled graciously. "As you can see, we're not wealthy ourselves. An extravagant ceremony would only make us feel awkward. As long as you have real affection for her and you're serious about your work, that's all we ask."

Forgetting even to bow my head in reply, I gazed speechlessly out at the garden for some time. My eyes felt hot. I told myself I'd make this woman a devoted and dutiful son-in-law.

When I left, the young lady accompanied me to the

bus stop. As we walked along, I said, "Well, what do you think? Shall we continue the relationship a while longer?" Sheer affectation.

"No," she said, laughing, "I've had enough."

"Aren't there any questions you want to ask me?" I said. A confirmed fool.

"Yes."

I was resolved to answer with the plain truth any question she might choose to ask.

"Has snow fallen on Mount Fuji yet?"

That threw me.

"Yes, it has. On the summit ..." My words trailed off as I glanced up and spotted Fuji before us. It gave me an odd feeling. "What the hell? You can see Fuji from Kōfu. You trying to make a fool of me?" I was suddenly speaking like a hoodlum. "That was a stupid question. What kind of fool do you take me for?"

She looked down at the ground and giggled. "But you're staying at Misaka Pass, so I thought it wouldn't do not to ask about Fuji."

Strange girl, I thought.

When I got back from Kōfu, I found that my shoulders were so stiff I could hardly breathe.

"You know, you're lucky, Missus. Misaka Pass is a pretty good place after all. It's like coming back home."

After dinner, the proprietress and her little sister took turns pounding on my shoulders. The woman's fists were hard and penetrating, but the girl's were soft and had little effect. Harder, harder, I kept saying, until at last she got a stick of firewood and whacked on my shoulders with that. That's what it took to relieve the tension, so keyed up and intent on my purpose had I been in Kōfu.

For two or three days after that I was distracted and had little will to work; I sat at my desk and scribbled aimlessly, smoked seven or eight packs of Golden Bat cigarettes, lay around doing nothing, sang "Even a Diamond, Unpolished" to myself over and over, and didn't write so much as a page of the novel I'd been working on.

"You haven't been doing so well since you went to Kōfu, have you, sir?" One morning as I sat at the desk with my chin propped up on my hand, my eyes closed, turning all sorts of things over in my mind, the fifteen-year-old sister, who was wiping the floor in the alcove behind me, said these words with a tone of sincere regret, and a touch of bitterness.

Without turning to look at her, I said, "Is that so? I haven't been doing so well, eh?"

"No, you haven't," she said, still wiping the floor. "The last two or three days you haven't gotten any work done at all, have you? Every morning, you know, I gather up all the pages you've written and left lying around, and put them in order. I really enjoy doing that, and I'm glad when you've written a lot. I came up here last night to peek in and see how you were doing—did you know that? You were lying on your futon with the quilt pulled up over your head."

I was grateful to her for those words. This may be overstating it a bit, but to me her concern seemed the purest form of support and encouragement for one making every effort to go on living. She expected nothing in return. I thought her quite beautiful.

By the end of October, the autumn leaves had become dark and ugly, and then an overnight storm came along and left nothing behind but a bare, black, winter forest. Sightseers were few and far between now. Business dropped off, and occasionally the proprietress would go shopping in Funazu or Yoshida at the foot of the mountain, taking the six-year-old boy with her and leaving the girl and myself alone for the day in the quiet, deserted teahouse. On one such day I began to feel the tedium of sitting alone on the second floor and went outside for a stroll. I saw the girl in the back yard, washing clothes, went up to her, flashed a smile, and said, in a loud voice, "I'm so bored!" She hung her head, and when I peered at her face I got quite a start. She was nearly in tears and obviously terrified. Right, I thought, doing a grim about-face and stomping off along a narrow, leaf-covered path. I felt perfectly miserable.

I was careful from then on. Whenever the girl and I were alone in the place, I tried to stay in my room on the second floor. If a customer came, I would lumber downstairs, partially with the intention of watching out for the girl, and sit in one corner of the shop drinking tea. One day a bride, escorted by two elderly men in crested ceremonial kimonos and *haori* coats, arrived in a hired automobile. The girl was alone in the shop, so I came downstairs, sat in a chair in one corner, and smoked a cigarette. The bride was decked out in full wedding regalia: long kimono with an elaborate design on the skirt, obi sash of gold brocade, and white wedding hood. Not knowing how to receive such singular guests, the girl, after pouring tea for the three of them, retreated to my corner as if to hide behind me and stared silently at the bride. A day that comes but once in a lifetime ... No doubt the bride was from the other side of the mountain, on her way to be married to someone in Funazu or Yoshida, and had decided to rest at the top of the pass and gaze at Fuji. It made for a scene that, even to a casual observer, was provocatively romantic. In a little while the bride rose and quietly left the shop to stand near the edge of the cliff and take in the view at her leisure. She stood with her legs crossed—a bold pose. Awfully sure of herself, I was thinking, admiring her, Fuji and her, when suddenly she looked up at the summit and gave a great yawn.

"My!" Behind me, a small cry showed that the girl, too, had been quick to notice. Before long the bride got back in the car with her escorts and left, to scathing reviews.

"She's *used* to this, the hussy. Must be her second, no, at least her third time. The groom's down at the foot of the mountain waiting for her, no doubt, but she has them stop the car and gets out to look at Fuji. Don't tell me a woman getting married for the first time would have the nerve to do that."

"She yawned!" the girl eagerly concurred. "Stretching open that big mouth of hers ... She ought to be ashamed of herself. Whatever you do, sir, you mustn't marry anyone like that."

It hardly befitted a man of my years, but I blushed. My own wedding plans were progressing smoothly, thanks to a certain mentor of mine who was taking care of everything. The ceremony, a dignified if meager affair with only two or three close family friends attending, was to be held at this man's house, and I, for my part, felt almost like a child inspired and encouraged by the affection of others.

Once November arrived, the cold at Misaka became hard to bear. A stove was set up downstairs.

"You must be freezing on the second floor. Why don't you work down here, beside the stove?" the lady of the house suggested, but I find it impossible to work with people watching, and declined. She continued to worry about me, however, and one day she went to Yoshida and came back with a *kotatsu* for my room. Snuggling beneath the coverlet of that little footwarmer, I felt grateful from the bottom of my heart for the kindness of these people. But gazing at Fuji, which was already covered with two-thirds of its full winter cap of snow, and the desolate trees on the nearer mountains, I began to see the meaninglessness of enduring much more of the penetrating cold at Misaka Pass and decided it was time to head for the lowlands. The day before I left, I was sitting on a chair in the shop wearing two dotera, one over the other, and sipping cheap green tea, when a pair of intellectual-looking young women in winter overcoats—typists, I guessed—approached on foot from the direction of the tunnel. Shrieking with laughter about one thing or another, they suddenly caught sight of Fuji and stopped as dead in their tracks as if they'd been shot. After consulting each other in whispers, one of them, a fair-skinned girl wearing glasses, came up to me with a smile on her face and said, "Excuse me, would you snap a photo of us, please?"

This flustered me. I'm not very good with gadgets, and I haven't the least interest in photography. What's more, I presented such a squalid figure in those two dotera that even my hosts at the teahouse had laughed and said I looked a proper mountain bandit, so I was thrown into quite a panic to be asked to perform such a fashionable act by those two gay flowers from (I presumed) Tokyo. But then, rethinking the situation, it occurred to me that even as shabbily dressed as I was, a discerning observer might easily detect in me a certain sensitivity and sophistication that would indicate at least sufficient dexterity to manipulate the shutter of a camera, and, buoyed up by this reflection, I feigned nonchalance as I took the instrument, casually asked for a brief explanation of how to work it, and peered into the viewfinder, inwardly all atremble. In the middle of the lens stood Fuji, large and imposing, and below, in the foreground, were two little poppies—or so the girls appeared in their red overcoats. They put their arms around each other and looked at the camera with sober, solemn expressions. It all struck me as very funny, and my hands shook helplessly. Suppressing my laughter, I peered through the finder again, and the two poppies grew even more rigid and demure. I was having a difficult time aiming and finally swept the two girls out of the picture entirely, allowing Fuji, and Fuji alone, to fill the lens. Goodbye, Mount Fuji.

Thanks for everything. *Click*.

"Got it."

"Thank you!" they said in unison. They'd be surprised when they got back home and had the film developed: only Fuji filling the frame, and not a trace of themselves.

The next day I came down from Misaka Pass. I stayed the first night at a cheap inn in Kōfu, and the following morning I leaned against the battered railing that ran along the corridor there, looking up at Fuji, about one-third of which was visible behind the surrounding mountains. It looked like the flower of a Chinese lantern plant.

TRANSLATED BY RALPH McCARTHY

VILLON'S WIFE

I was awakened by the sound of the front door being flung open, but I did not get out of bed. I knew it could only be my husband returning dead-drunk in the middle of the night.

He switched on the light in the next room and, breathing very heavily, began to rummage through the drawers of the desk and the bookcase, as if he were searching for something. After a few minutes there was a noise that sounded as if he had flopped down on the floor. Then I could hear only his panting. Wondering what he might be up to, I called to him from where I lay, "Have you had supper yet? There's some cold rice in the cupboard."

"Thank you," he answered in an unaccustomedly gentle tone. "How is the boy? Does he still have a fever?"

This was also unusual. The boy is four this year, but whether because of malnutrition, or his father's alcoholism, or sickness, he is actually smaller than most two-year-olds. He is not even sure on his feet, and as for talking, it's all he can do to say "yum-yum" or "ugh." Sometimes I wonder if he is not feebleminded. Once, when I took him to the public bath and held him in my arms after undressing him, he looked so small and pitifully scrawny that my heart sank, and I burst into tears in front of everybody. The boy is always having upset stomachs or fevers, but my husband almost never spends any time at home, and I wonder what if anything he thinks about the child. If I should mention to him that the boy has a fever, he says, "You ought to take him to a doctor." Then he throws on his coat and goes off somewhere. I would like to take the boy to the doctor, but I don't have any money. There is nothing else I can do but lie beside him and stroke his head.

But that night, for whatever reason, my husband was strangely gentle, and for once asked me about the boy's fever. It didn't make me happy. I felt instead a kind of premonition of something terrible, and cold chills ran up and down my spine. I couldn't think of anything to say, so I lay there in silence. For a while there was no other sound but my husband's furious panting.

Then there came from the front entrance the thin voice of a woman, "Is anyone at home?" I shuddered all over as if icy water had been poured over me.

"Are you at home, Mr. Otani?" This time there was a somewhat sharp inflection to her voice. She slid the door open and called in a definitely angry voice, "Mr. Otani. Why don't you answer?"

My husband at last went to the door. "Well, what is it?" he asked in a frightened, stupid tone.

"You know perfectly well what it is," the woman said, lowering her voice. "What makes you steal other people's money when you've got a nice home like this? Stop your inhuman joking and give it back. If you don't, I'm going straight to the police."

"I don't know what you're talking about. I won't stand for your insults. You've got no business coming here. Get out! If you don't get out, I'll be the one to call the police."

There came the voice of another man, "I must say, you've got your nerve, Mr. Otani. What do you mean we have no business coming here? You really dumbfound me. This time is serious. It's going beyond the limits of a joke when you steal other people's money. Heaven only knows all my wife and I have suffered on account of you. And on top of everything else you do something as low as you did tonight. Mr. Otani, I misjudged you."

"It's blackmail," my husband angrily exclaimed in a shaking voice. "It's extortion. Get out! If you've got any complaints I'll listen to them tomorrow."

"What a revolting thing to say. You really are an out-and-out scoundrel. I have no alternative but to call the police."

There was in his words a hatred so terrible that I went gooseflesh all over.

"Go to hell," my husband shouted, but his voice had already weakened and sounded hollow.

I got up, threw a wrap over my nightgown, and went to the front hall. I bowed to the two visitors. A round-faced man of about fifty wearing a knee-length overcoat asked, "Is this your wife?" and, without a trace of a smile, faintly inclined his head in my direction as if he were nodding.

The woman was a thin, small person of about forty, neatly dressed. She loosened her shawl and, also un-smiling, returned my bow with the words, "Excuse us for breaking in this way in the middle of the night."

My husband suddenly slipped on his sandals and made for the door. The man grabbed his arm and the two of them struggled for a moment. "Let go or I'll stab you!" my husband shouted, a jackknife flashing in his right hand. The knife was a pet possession of his, and I remembered that he usually kept it in his desk drawer. When he got home he must have been expecting trouble, and the knife was what he had been searching for.

The man shrank back and in the interval my husband, flapping the sleeves of his coat like a huge crow, bolted outside.

"Thief!" the man shouted and started to pursue him, but I ran to the front gate in my bare feet and clung to him.

"Please don't. It won't help for either of you to get hurt. I will take the responsibility for everything."

The woman said, "Yes, she's right. You can never tell what a lunatic will do."

"Swine! It's the police this time! I can't stand any more." The man stood there staring emptily at the darkness outside and muttering as if to himself. But the force had gone out of his body.

"Please come in and tell me what has happened. I may be able to settle whatever the matter is. The place is a mess, but please come in."

The two visitors exchanged glances and nodded slightly to one another. The man said, with a changed expression, "I'm afraid that whatever you may say our minds are already made up. But it might be a good idea to tell you, Mrs. Otani, all that has happened."

"Please do come in and stay for a while."

"I'm afraid we won't be able to stay long." So saying, the man started to remove his overcoat.

"Please keep your coat on. It's very cold here, and I don't have any heating in the house."

"Well then, if you will forgive me."

"Please, both of you."

The man and the woman entered my husband's room. They seemed appalled by the desolation of what they saw. The mats looked as though they were rotting, the paper doors were in shreds, the walls were beginning to fall in, and the paper had peeled away from the storage closet, revealing the framework within. In a corner were a desk and a bookcase—an empty bookcase.

I offered the two visitors some torn cushions from which the stuffing leaked, and said, "Please sit on the cushions—the mats are so dirty." And I bowed to them again. "I must apologize for all the trouble my husband seems to have been causing you, and for the terrible exhibition he put on tonight, for whatever reason it was. He has such a peculiar disposition." I choked in the middle of my words and burst into tears.

"Excuse me for asking, Mrs. Otani, but how old are you?" the man asked. He was sitting cross-legged on the torn cushion, with his elbows on his knees, propping up his chin with his fists. As he asked the question he leaned forward toward me.

"I am twenty-six."

"Is that all you are? I suppose that's only natural, considering your husband's about thirty, but it amazes me all the same."

The woman, showing her face from behind the man's

back, said, "I couldn't help wondering, when I came in and saw what a fine wife he has, why Mr. Otani behaves the way he does."

"He's sick. That's what it is. He didn't use to be that way, but he keeps getting worse." He gave a great sigh, then continued, "Mrs. Otani. My wife and I run a little restaurant near the Nakano station. We both originally came from the country, but I got fed up with dealing with penny-pinching farmers, and came to Tokyo with my wife. After the usual series of hardships and breaks, we managed to save up a little and, along about 1936, opened a cheap little restaurant catering to customers with at most one or two yen to spend at one time for entertainment. By not going in for luxuries and working like slaves, we managed to lay in quite a stock of whiskey and gin. When liquor got short and plenty of other drinking establishments went out of business, we were able to keep going.

"The war with America and England broke out, but even after the bombings got pretty severe, we didn't feel like being evacuated to the country, not having any children to tie us down. We figured that we might as well stick to our business until the place got burnt down. Your husband first started coming to our place in the spring of 1944, as I recall. We were not yet losing the war, or if we were we didn't know how things actually stood, and we thought that if we could just hold out for another two or three years we could somehow get peace on terms of equality. When Mr. Otani first appeared in our shop, he was not alone. It's a little embarrassing to tell you about it, but I might as well come out with the whole story and not keep anything from you. Your husband sneaked in by the kitchen door along with an older woman. I forgot to say that along about that time the front door of our place was shut every day, and only a few regular customers got in by the back door.

"This older woman lived in the neighborhood, and when the bar where she worked was closed and she lost her job, she often came here with her men-friends. That's why we weren't particularly surprised when your husband crept in by the kitchen door with this older woman, whose name was Akichan. I took them to the back room and brought out some gin. Mr. Otani drank his liquor very quietly that evening. Akichan paid the bill and the two of them left together by the back door. It's odd, but I can't forget how strangely gentle and refined he behaved that night. I wonder if when the devil makes his first appearance in somebody's house he acts in such a lonely and melancholy way.

"From that night on Mr. Otani was a steady customer. Ten days later he came alone and all of a sudden produced a hundred-yen note. At that time a hundred yen was a lot of money, more than two or three thousand yen today. He pressed the money into my hand and wouldn't take no for an answer. 'Take care of it please,' he said, smiling timidly. He looked as if he had already been drinking quite a bit, but, as you know, no man can hold his liquor like he can. Just when you think he's drunk, he suddenly becomes serious and engages in a perfectly rational conversation. No matter how much he drinks I have never seen him unsteady on his feet. They say that a man around thirty is in the prime of life and can hold his liquor best, but it is very rare to find anyone like Mr. Otani. That night he seemed to have drunk quite a bit before he came, and at my place he downed ten glasses of gin as fast as I could set them up. All this was almost entirely without a word. My wife and I tried to start a conversation, but all he did was smile rather shamefacedly and nod vaguely. Suddenly he asked the time and got up. 'What about the change?' I called after him. 'That's all right,' he said. 'I don't know what to do with it,' I insisted, to which he smiled wryly and said, 'Please save it until the next time. I'll be coming back.' He went out. Mrs. Otani, that was the one and only time that we ever got any money from him. Since then he has always put us off with one excuse or another, and for three years he has managed without paying a penny to drink up all our liquor almost without assistance."

Before I knew what I was doing I burst out laughing. It all seemed so funny to me, although I can't explain why. I covered my mouth in confusion, but when I looked at the lady I saw that she was also laughing unaccountably, and then her husband could not help but laugh too.

"No, it is really no laughing matter, but I'm so fed up that I feel like laughing. Really, if he used all his ability in some other direction, he could become a cabinet minister or a Ph.D. or anything else he wanted. When Akichan was still friends with Mr. Otani she used to brag about him all the time. First of all, she said, he came from a terrific family. He was the younger son of Baron Otani. It is true that he had been disinherited because of his conduct, but when his father, the present baron, died, he and his elder brother were to divide the estate. He was brilliant, a genius in fact. In spite of his youth he was the best poet in Japan. What's more, he was a great scholar, who had gone from the Peers' School to the First High School and the Tokyo Imperial University. He was a perfect demon at German and French. To hear Akichan talk, he was a kind of god, and the funny thing was that she didn't make it all up. Other people also said that he was the younger son of Baron Otani and a famous poet. As a result even my wife, who is getting along in years, was as wild about him as Akichan. She used to tell me what a difference it makes when people have been well brought up. And the way she pined for him to come was quite unbearable. They say the day of the nobility is over, but until the war ended I can tell you that nobody had his way with the women like that disinherited son of the aristocracy. It was unbelievable how they fell for him. I suppose it was what people would nowadays call 'slave mentality.'

"For my part, I'm a man, and at that a very cool sort of man, and I don't think that some little peer—if you will pardon the expression—some member of the country gentry who is only a younger son, is all that different from myself. I never for a moment got worked up about him in so sickening a way. But all the same, that gentleman was my weak spot. No matter how firmly I resolved not to give him any liquor the next time, when he suddenly appeared at some unexpected hour, looking like a hunted man, and I saw how relieved he was at last to have reached our place, my resolution weakened, and I ended up by giving him the liquor. Even when he got drunk he never made any special nuisance of himself, and if only he had paid the bill he would have been a good customer. He never advertised himself and didn't take any silly pride in being a genius or anything of the sort. When Akichan or somebody else would sit beside him and sound off to us about his greatness, he would either change the subject completely or say, 'I want some money so I can pay the bill,' throwing a wet blanket over everything.

"The war finally ended. We started openly doing business in black-market liquor and put new curtains in front of the place. For all its seediness the shop looked rather lively, and we hired a girl to lend some charm. Then who should show up again but that damned gentleman. He no longer brought women with him, but always came in the company of two or three newspaper and magazine writers. He was drinking even more than before, and used to get very wild-looking. He began to come out with really vulgar jokes, which he had never done before, and sometimes for no good reason he would strike one of the reporters he brought with him or would start a fistfight. What's more, he seduced the twenty-year-old girl who was working in our place. We were really dumbfounded, but there was nothing we could do about it at that stage, and we had no choice but to let the matter drop. We advised the girl to resign herself to it, and quietly sent her back to her parents. I begged Mr. Otani not to come any more, but he answered in a threatening tone, 'People who make money on the black market have no business criticizing others. I know all about you.' The next night be showed up as if nothing had happened.

"Maybe it was by way of punishment for the black-market business we had been doing that we had to take such a monster on our hands. But what he did tonight can't be passed over just because he's a poet or a gentleman. It was plain robbery. He stole 5,000 yen from us. Nowadays all our money goes for stock, and we are lucky if we have 500 or 1,000 yen in the place. The reason why we had as much as 5,000 yen tonight was that I had made an end-of-the-year round of our regular customers and managed to collect that much. If I don't hand the money over to the wholesalers immediately, we won't be able to stay in business. That's how much it means to us. Well, my wife was going over the accounts in the back room and had put the money in the cupboard drawer. He was drinking by himself out in front but seems to have noticed what she did. Suddenly he got up, went straight to the back room, and without a word pushed my wife aside and opened the drawer. He grabbed the 5,000 yen in bills and stuffed them in his pocket.

"We rushed into the shop, still speechless with amazement, and then out into the street. I shouted for him to stop, and the two of us ran after him. For a minute I felt like screaming 'Thief!' and getting the people in the street to join us, but after all Mr. Otani is an old acquaintance, and I couldn't be too harsh on him. I made up my mind that I would not let him out of my sight. I would follow him wherever he went, and when I saw that he had quieted down, I would calmly ask for the money. We are only small business people, and when we finally caught up with him here, we had no choice but to suppress our feelings and politely ask him to return the money. And then what happened? He took out a knife and threatened to stab me! What a thing to happen!"

Again the whole thing seemed so funny to me, for reasons I can't explain, that I burst out laughing. The lady turned red, and smiled a little. I couldn't stop laughing. Even though I knew that it would have a bad effect on the proprietor, it all seemed so strangely funny that I laughed until the tears came. I suddenly wondered if the phrase "the great laugh at the end of the world" that occurs in one of my husband's poems didn't mean something of the sort.

And yet it was not a matter that could be settled just by laughing about it. I thought for a minute and said, "Somehow or other I will make things good, if you will only wait one more day before you report to the police. I'll call on you tomorrow without fail." I carefully inquired where the restaurant was and begged them to consent. They agreed to let things stand for the time being, and left. Then I sat by myself in the middle of the cold room trying to think of a plan. Nothing came to me. I stood up, took off my wrap, and crept in among the covers where my boy was sleeping. As I stroked his head I thought how wonderful it would be if the night never never ended.

My father used to keep a stall in Asakusa Park. My mother died when I was young, and my father and I lived by ourselves in a tenement. We ran the stall together. My husband used to come now and then, and before long I was meeting him at other places without my father's knowing it. When I became pregnant I persuaded him to treat me as his wife, although it wasn't officially registered, of course. Now the boy is growing up fatherless, while my husband goes off for three or four nights or even for a whole month at a time. I don't know where he goes or what he does. When he comes back he is always soused, and he sits there, deathly pale, breathing heavily and staring at my face. Sometimes he cries and the tears stream down his face, or without warning he crawls into my bed and holds me tightly. "Oh it can't go on. I'm afraid. I'm afraid. Help me!"

Sometimes he trembles all over, and even after he falls asleep he talks deliriously and moans. The next morning he is absentminded, like a man with the soul taken out of him. Then he disappears and doesn't return for three or four nights. A couple of my husband's publisher friends have been looking after the boy and myself for some time, and once in a while they bring enough money to keep us from starving.

I dozed off, then opened my eyes before I was aware of it to see the morning light pouring in through the cracks in the shutters. I got up, dressed, strapped the boy to my back and went outside. I felt as if I couldn't stand being in the silent house another minute.

I set out aimlessly and found myself walking in the direction of the station. I bought a bun at an outdoor stand and fed it to the boy. On a sudden impulse I bought a ticket for Kichijoji and got on the tram. While I stood hanging from a strap I happened to notice a poster with my husband's name on it. It was an advertisement for a magazine in which he had published a story called "François Villon." While I stared at the title "François Villon" and at my husband's name, painful tears sprang from my eyes, why I can't say, and the poster clouded over so I couldn't see it.

I got off at Kichijoji and, for the first time in I don't know how many years, I walked in the park. The cypresses around the pond had all been cut down, and the place looked like a construction site. It was strangely bare and cold, not at all as it used to be.

I took the boy off my back and the two of us sat on a broken bench next to the pond. I fed the boy a sweet potato I had brought from home. "It's a pretty pond, isn't it? There used to be many carp and goldfish, but now there aren't any left. It's too bad, isn't it?"

I don't know what he thought. He just laughed oddly with his mouth full of sweet potato. Even if he is my own child, he did give me the feeling almost of an idiot.

I couldn't settle anything just by sitting there on the bench, so I put the boy on my back and returned slowly to the station. I bought a ticket for Nakano. Without thought or plan, I boarded the tram as though I were being sucked into a horrible whirlpool. I got off at Nakano and followed the directions to the restaurant.

The front door would not open. I went around to the back and entered by the kitchen door. The owner was away, and his wife was cleaning the shop by herself. As soon as I saw her I began to pour out lies of which I did not imagine myself capable.

"It looks as if I'll be able to pay you back every bit of the money tomorrow, if not tonight. There's nothing for you to worry about."

"Oh, how wonderful. Thank you so much." She looked almost happy, but still there remained on her face a shadow of uneasiness, as if she were not yet satisfied.

"It's true. Someone will bring the money here without fail. Until he comes I'm to stay here as your hostage. Is that guarantee enough for you? Until the money comes I'll be glad to help around the shop."

I took the boy off my back and let him play by himself. He is accustomed to playing alone and doesn't get in the way at all. Perhaps because he's stupid, he's not afraid of strangers, and he smiled happily at the madam. While I was away getting the rationed goods for her, she gave him some empty American cans to play with, and when I got back he was in a corner of the room, banging the cans and rolling them on the floor.

About noon the boss returned from his marketing. As soon as I caught sight of him I burst out with the same lies I had told the madam. He looked amazed. "Is that a fact? All the same, Mrs. Otani, you can't be sure of money until you've got it in your hands." He spoke in a surprisingly calm, almost explanatory tone.

"But it's really true. Please have confidence in me and wait just this one day before you make it public. In the meantime I'll help in the restaurant."

"If the money is returned, that's all I ask," the boss said, almost to himself. "There are five or six days left to the end of the year, aren't there?"

"Yes and so, you see, I mean—oh, some customers have come. Welcome!" I smiled at the three customers—they looked like workmen—who had entered the shop, and whispered to the madam, "Please lend me an apron."

One of the customers called out, "Say, you've hired a beauty. She's terrific."

"Don't lead her astray," the boss said, in a tone which wasn't altogether joking. "She cost a lot of money."

"A million dollar thoroughbred?" another customer coarsely joked.

"They say that even in thoroughbreds the female costs only half price," I answered in the same coarse way, while putting the sake on to warm.

"Don't be modest! From now on in Japan there's equality of the sexes, even for horses and dogs," the youngest customer roared. "Sweetheart, I've fallen in love. It's love at first sight. But is that your kid over there?"

"No," said the madam, carrying the boy in her arms from the back room. "We got this child from our relatives. At last we have an heir."

"What'll you leave him beside your money?" a customer teased.

The boss with a dark expression muttered, "A love affair and debts." Then, changing his tone, "What'll you have? How about a mixed grill?"

It was Christmas Eve. That must be why there was such a steady stream of customers. I had scarcely eaten a thing since morning, but I was so upset that I refused even when the madam urged me to have a bite. I just went on flitting around the restaurant lightly as a ballerina. Maybe it is just conceit, but the shop seemed exceptionally lively that night, and there were quite a few customers who wanted to know my name or tried to shake my hand.

But I didn't have the slightest idea how it would all end. I went on smiling and answering the customers' dirty jokes with even dirtier jokes in the same vein, slipping from customer to customer, pouring the drinks. Before long I got to thinking that I would just as soon my body melted and flowed away like ice cream.

It seems as if miracles sometimes do happen even in this world. A little after nine a man entered, wearing a tricornered paper Christmas hat and a black mask which covered the upper part of his face. He was followed by an attractive woman of slender build who looked thirty-four or thirty-five. The man sat on a chair in the corner with his back to me, but as soon as he came in I knew who it was. It was my thief of a husband.

He sat there without seeming to pay any attention to

me. I also pretended not to recognize him, and went on joking with the other customers. The lady seated opposite my husband called me to their table. My husband stared at me from beneath his mask, as if surprised in spite of himself. I lightly patted his shoulder and asked, "Aren't you going to wish me a merry Christmas? What do you say? You look as if you've already put away a quart or two."

The lady ignored this. She said, "I have something to discuss with the proprietor. Would you mind calling him here for a moment?"

I went to the kitchen, where the boss was frying fish. "Otani has come back. Please go and see him, but don't tell the woman he's with anything about me. I don't want to embarrass him."

"So he really has come after all?" The proprietor had half doubted my lies, and yet he seemed nevertheless to have placed quite a bit of trust in them. Now he simply had concluded that my husband had returned as the result of some instigation on my part.

"Please don't say anything about me," I repeated.

"If that's the way you want it, it's all right with me," he consented easily, and went out front. After a quick look around the restaurant, the boss walked straight to the table where my husband was. The beautiful lady exchanged two or three words with him, and the three of them left the shop.

It was all over. Everything had been settled. Somehow I had believed all along that it would be, and I felt exhilarated. I seized the wrist of a young customer in a dark-blue suit, a boy not more than twenty, and I cried, "Drink up! Drink up! It's Christmas!"

In just thirty minutes—no, it was even sooner than that, so soon it startled me, the boss returned alone. "Mrs. Otani, I want to thank you. I've got the money back."

"I'm so glad. All of it?"

He answered with a funny smile, "All he took yesterday."

"And how much does the rest of what he owes you come to altogether? Roughly—an absolute minimum."

"Twenty thousand yen."

"Does that cover it?"

"It's a minimum."

"I'll make it good. Will you employ me starting tomorrow? I'll pay it back by working."

"What! You're joking!" And we laughed together.

Tonight I left the restaurant after ten and returned to the house with the boy. As I expected, my husband was not at home, but that didn't bother me. Tomorrow when I go to the restaurant I may see him again, for all I know. Why has such a good plan never occurred to me before? All the suffering I have gone through has been because of my own stupidity. I was always quite a success at entertaining the customers at my father's stall, and I'll certainly get to be pretty skillful at the restaurant. As a matter of fact, I received about 500 yen in tips tonight.

From the following day on my life changed completely. I became lighthearted and gay. The first thing I did was to go to a beauty parlor and have a permanent. I bought cosmetics and mended my dresses. I felt as though the worries that had weighed so heavily on me had been completely wiped away.

In the morning I get up and eat breakfast with the boy. Then I put him on my back and leave for work. New Year's is the big season at the restaurant, and I've been so busy my eyes swim. My husband comes in for a drink about once every two days. He lets me pay the bill and then disappears again. Quite often he looks in on the shop late at night and asks if it isn't time for me to be going home. Then we return pleasantly together.

"Why didn't I do this from the start? It's brought me such happiness."

"Women don't know anything about happiness or un-happiness."

"Perhaps not. What about men?"

"Men only have unhappiness. They are always fighting fear."

"I don't understand. I only know I wish this life could go on forever. The boss and the madam are such nice people."

"Don't be silly. They're grasping country bumpkins. They make me drink because they think they'll make money out of it in the end."

"That's their business. You can't blame them for it. But that's not the whole story is it? You had an affair with the madam, didn't you?"

"A long time ago. Does the old guy realize it?"

"I'm sure he does. I heard him say with a sigh that you had brought him a seduction and debts."

"I must seem a horrible character to you, but the fact is that I want to die so badly I can't stand it. Ever since I was born I have been thinking of nothing but dying. It would be better for everyone concerned if I were dead, that's certain. And yet I can't seem to die. There's something strange and frightening, like God, which won't let me die."

"That's because you have your work."

"My work doesn't mean a thing. I don't write either masterpieces or failures. If people say something is good, it becomes good. If they say it's bad, it becomes bad. But what frightens me is that somewhere in the world there is a God. There is, isn't there?"

"I don't have any idea."

Now that I have worked twenty days at the restaurant I realize that every last one of the customers is a criminal. I have come to think that my husband is very much on the mild side compared to them. And I see now that not only the customers but everyone you meet walking in the streets is hiding some crime. A beautifully dressed lady came to the door selling sake at 300 yen the quart. That was cheap, considering what prices are nowadays, and the madam snapped it up. It turned out to be watered. I thought that in a world where even such an aristocratic-looking lady is forced to resort to such tricks, it is impossible that anyone alive has a clear conscience.

God, if you exist, show yourself to me! Toward the end of the New Year season I was raped by a customer. It was raining that night, and it didn't seem likely that my husband would appear. I got ready to go, even though one customer was still left. I picked up the boy, who was sleeping in a corner of the back room, and put him on my back. "I'd like to borrow your umbrella again," I said to the madam.

"I've got an umbrella. I'll take you home," said the last customer, getting up as if he meant it. He was a short, thin man about twenty-five, who looked like a factory worker. It was the first time he had been a customer since I was working in the restaurant.

"It's very kind of you, but I am accustomed to walking by myself."

"You live a long way off, I know. I come from the same neighborhood. I'll take you back. Bill, please." He had only had three glasses and didn't seem particularly drunk.

We boarded the tram together and got off at my stop. Then we walked in the falling rain side by side under the same umbrella through the pitch-dark streets. The young man, who up to this point hadn't said a word, began to talk in a lively way. "I know all about you. You see, I'm a fan of Mr. Otani's and I also write poetry myself. I was hoping to show him some of my work before long, but he intimidates me so."

We had reached my house. "Thank you very much," I said, "I'll see you again at the restaurant."

"Goodbye," the young man said, going off into the rain.

I was wakened in the middle of the night by the noise of the front gate being opened. I thought that it was my husband returning, drunk as usual, so I lay there without saying anything.

A man's voice called, "Mrs. Otani, excuse me for bothering you."

I got up, put on the light, and went to the front entrance. The young man was there, staggering so badly he could scarcely stand.

"Excuse me, Mrs. Otani. On the way back I stopped for another drink and, to tell the truth, I live at the other end of town, and when I got to the station the last tram had already left. Mrs. Otani, would you please let me spend the night here? I don't need any blankets or anything else. I'll be glad to sleep here in the front hall until the first tram leaves tomorrow morning. If it wasn't raining I'd sleep outdoors somewhere in the neighborhood, but it's hopeless with this rain. Please let me stay."

"My husband isn't at home, but if the front hall will do, please stay." I got the two torn cushions and gave them to him.

"Thanks very much. Oh, I've had too much to drink," he said with a groan. He lay down just as he was in the front hall, and by the time I got back to bed I could already hear his snores.

The next morning at dawn without ceremony he took me.

That day I went to the restaurant with my boy as usual, acting as if nothing had happened. My husband was sitting at a table reading a newspaper, a glass of liquor beside him. I thought how pretty the morning sunshine looked, sparkling on the glass.

"Isn't anybody here," I asked. He looked up from his paper. "The boss hasn't come back yet from marketing. The madam was in the kitchen just a minute ago. Isn't she there now?"

"You didn't come last night, did you?"

"I did come. It's got so that I can't get to sleep without a look at my favorite waitress's face. I dropped in after ten but they said you had just left."

"And then?"

"I spent the night here. It was raining so hard."

"I may be sleeping here from now on."

"That's a good idea, I suppose."

"Yes, that's what I'll do. There's no sense in renting the house forever."

My husband didn't say anything but turned back to his paper. "Well, what do you know. They're writing bad things about me again. They call me a fake aristocrat with Epicurean leanings. That's not true. It would be more correct to refer to me as an Epicurean in terror of God. Look! It says here that I'm a monster. That's not true, is it? It's a little late, but I'll tell you now why I took the 5,000 yen. It was so that I might give you and the boy the first happy New Year in a long time. That proves I'm not a monster, doesn't it?"

His words didn't make me especially glad. I said, "There's nothing wrong with being a monster, is there? As long as we can stay alive."

TRANSLATED BY DONALD KEENE